hard cash

"Slick, cool and compulsive, *Hard Cash* is pumped full of adrenaline as Rich discovers life in the fast lane. You'll enjoy the ride."
Telegraph

"zappy, intelligent"
The Times

"shrewd, well–paced, enjoyable novel . . . scenes are vividly caught . . . a good read"
Books for Keeps

shacked up

"incredible impact and an undeniable realism . . . direct, immediate and credible . . . I only hope there will be a third"
Bookseller

"Original, inventive and very funny – definitely worth reading"
Daily Telegraph

footloose

"a perfect holiday read, full of sun, sand and saucy bits!"
Sugar

Have you read the first
two books in this trilogy?

Hard Cash
Shacked Up

And look out for other
books by Kate Cann:

Footloose
Fiesta
Shop Dead